This igloo book belongs to:

....

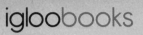

Published in 2015
by Igloo Books Ltd
Cottage Farm
Sywell
NN6 0BJ
www.igloobooks.com

HUN001 0415
2 4 6 8 10 9 7 5 3 1
ISBN 978-1-78440-939-5

Written by Melanie Joyce
Illustrated by Polona Lovšin

Printed and manufactured in China

I Love You, Daddy

Melanie Joyce

Polona Lovšin

I love you, Daddy,
because you make me fly...

...Up to the clouds, like a bird in the sky.

Wherever you go,
I come along, too.
There's always adventure
when I follow you.

When I ask you to play,
you say that you will.
We have so much fun
when we roll down the hill.

Daddy, I love you
because when I cry,
you hold my sore paw
and wipe my tears dry.

When we go paddling in the cool river's swish,
we wait patiently to catch wriggly fish.

I love it, Daddy,
when you creep to the tree
and bring back yummy,
sticky honey for me.

When you swim,
I come along for the ride.

You carry me safely
to the other side.

I love it when we splash
in rainy puddles.
You hold out your arms and say,
"Time for cuddles!"

You carry me home in the soft evening light.
I feel so safe as you hold me tight.

Daddy, I know that you love me through and through.
You are so special to me and I love you, too.

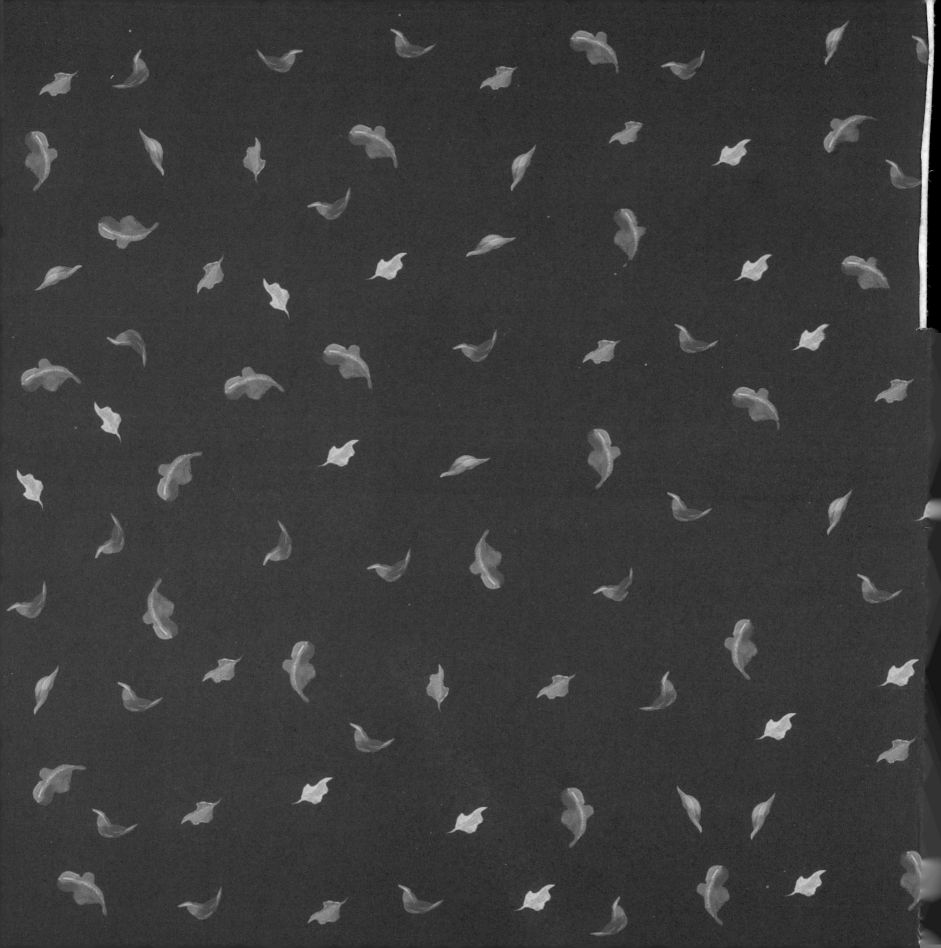